MW01106164

Our $STARLAND$

© Emily Holton, 2008
First Edition

Edited by Andy Brown and Maya Merrick
Drawings from a found astronomy binder (A. Pring, 119-9C)

Many thanks to Andy Brown and Maya Merrick, for everything.
The author would like to acknowledge the influence of Lucien Malson's book *Wolf Children*, as well as J. J. Rousseau and Maurice Merleau-Ponty's essays and lectures on feral children.

Library and Archives Canada Cataloguing in Publication

Holton, Emily, 1980-
     Dear Canada Council ; Our starland / Emily Holton.

Two novellas, with illustrations, on inverted pages.
ISBN 978-1-894994-36-1

     I. Title. II. Title: Our starland.

PS8615.O482D32 2008   C813'.6   C2008-905849-6

Dépot Legal, Bibliothèque nationale du Québec
Printed and bound in Canada. Distributed by Litdistco: 1-800-591-6250

conundrum press
PO Box 55003, CSP Fairmount, Montreal, Quebec, H2T 3E2, Canada
conpress@ican.net   www.conundrumpress.com

conundrum press acknowledges the financial assistance of the Canada Council for the Arts toward our publishing program.

Canada Council for the Arts   **Conseil des Arts du Canada**

The author would like to recognize the support of the Province of Nova Scotia through the Department of Tourism, Culture and Heritage.

Our STARLAND

Emily Holton

a conundrum reversible book

ONE

1

Elbows on the paint-chipped sill and her chin in her hands, Willa watches the pickers light fires. She pulls the chain to turn out her little glass reading light and counts, by their cigarettes, fifteen.

2

R: Did you pray this morning, darling, like I showed you?
A: [...]
R: That's all right, my love. It is up to you to answer His prayers. Not He to answer yours.

— Transcription from case file 87-479, St. Veronica's House, May 1993

3

The sun is low, and the light is bending. Vancouver breathes through its mouth a flume of steel cars, lucent faces and hands, teeth, tufts of hair. Sundogs in the sky. Almost dusk. Almost dusk and by now you are so tired in your mind you can barely stand upright. Almost dusk and it's nothing now but the speed and the stench of the cars throwing wind and the smoke and the yellow hair; the rear-views, the white lines, and all the rest that's ignited by sunlight, brakelight, window glass, sky. Keep your eyes in the ditch. Keep your hand like she showed you. You want Raye, but she's gone.

You want Raye.

4

Beyond Willa's third floor window is the big driveway, then the barn, then the field where the pickers sleep. After that are apple trees, little rows, hundreds and hundreds of them and she can see them all the way back to where the hills start tonight. Each one of them grown tight onto their wires, nice and flat, so the pickers can strip them of every last flicker. Put it all in trucks, and send it away.

Eleven, and perfect, she keeps her bed by the window. She knows the difference, from here, between the glow of guitar wood and a beer bottle flash; between the wood smoke and sage smoke as they come up on the wind. Willa can't see them, just the stars of their cigarettes, but she can picture them. Their faces tanned, their frames narrow. They have always come. Behind them, in line at the tractor in the morning, Willa inspects without meaning to their dreadlocks and peeling shoulders, their dirty feet.

5

Levi takes one hand off the wheel and reaches for a pouch of Player's Special Cut tobacco, three-quarters full and held closed by a pink hair elastic. He pulls some papers from the sun visor, takes one, and replaces the rest of the pack above his head.

There is no good radio anywhere anymore.

6

It's August, and in the Okanagan Valley the season for apples is just beginning. Here, the summer is very hot. This July the desert brush all lit on fire — it happens sometimes, in the day. But at night, all is quiet. Pickers everywhere, all the time, and none of them much older than her.

They live here for now, and on hundreds of other farms in this valley; they hitchhike, smoke cigarettes, and line the curbs of gas stations, waiting for showers. Levi's farm has its own shed with showers in it, and another with a stove. He pays the highest too, even Willa knows that.

They don't talk to her.

7

Levi slows for construction and, suddenly, there is more street light falling than sun. Maybe she doesn't need to sleep. Maybe he dreams them anyways, the little sounds of her. Little brown feet on the hardwood stairs, little slaps like a lit match in water. The flutter and flannelette sigh of her; the fridge door, a bowl and spoon. Maybe she's already had all the dreams that she needs to have, when she was a baby, or before she was born.

On his right, a welder's arc flashes and Levi's hands flicker white, but he's looking at the windshield glass — something in there. He lifts a hand to touch it. White again.

8

Takes delight in the sound of piano but is insensitive to the sound of a ticking clock.

— Notes from patient care plan re: Audric Parent, 1989, St. Veronica's House

9

Tent to tent to trailer, and back again. Six more of them coming up the driveway now, laughing, and they pass on their way back to their tents and trailers; back to their vans and their shepherd dogs. Back from wherever that dark road leads. The hills behind will be bright red and beautiful in the daylight but at night they grow bigger, blacker than the sky.

10

He scratched in the dirt with his fingernails and, for months, appeared interested only in food. They marvelled at his opacity. He knew nothing, they said. Nothing of the world.

— From "Seven Years," by Rayline Ulyrk, *Child Development*, edition 14, volume 33 (1996)

11

Shining through the glass is the faintest imprint of a wing, every feather. He can't remember it happening, but there it is.

TWO

12

R: Your only father is the Heavenly Father, Audric.
A: […]
R: Do you know who your mother is, love?
A: […]
R: I believe that it was her will that brought you to us, I do.

— Transcription from case file 87-479, St. Veronica's House, August 1989

13

Heat lighting, and sleep coming. Levi takes a last haul and feeds his smoke to the windstream to his left, and watches the side-view as the heater explodes. Squints and rubs his face with both hands. The truth is, her mother never slept either.

14

Willa crawls back to her pillow, lies on her back, and whispers: Now I will dream of being a baby.

But she doesn't.

15

Even from the road. Even though it's dark now, you can see as he passes that his eyes are light blue and bright in their sockets. First thing. Eyes blue as a man's who has planted a flag at both poles. But that's not what you think of when you see them.

You think, Run.

16

Her mother knew the constellations, and Willa can remember some. She taught Willa when Willa was just a baby. Miguel and the Swan, and the Great Bear and His Bow. She learned from her mother that the stars are always sliding in one direction, *that* way, beyond the barn, and the fires, and the tents where the pickers sleep.

Across the hall, his door is closed. There's no one in there but it's okay. And anyways, it doesn't matter. She'll go downstairs either way, and she'll open that door whether he's home or not. This time, maybe, she won't even need the porch light. She can see.

17

When they ripped the wild boy of Mount Currie from the forest he walked so like an animal that the only way to erect him was by pieces of wood tied to his legs. These he resisted, sometimes with his teeth.

— From "Seven Years," by Rayline Ulyrk, *Child Development*, edition 14, volume 33 (1996)

18

Gravel pops and he's stopped for you. Run.

19

Confuses dreams and reality in storytelling exercises. Imperceptive to changes in temperature.

— From St. Veronica's House patient care plan letter re: Audric Parent, 1995

20

"You looking for work?"

21

Hands like yours, but they open better. Hands like yours, but stronger. Bark brown and climbing with veins like yours too, climbing up to the shoulder, to the ear, and the thin, grey chest pressing back in on itself.

"You looking for work, kid, or what?"

22

Only dark down the hall and Willa slides in. Slides on the dirty, calloused soles of her feet down the stairs to the kitchen. For a moment, she allows herself the half-light of the freezer. Her breath clouding into slow, supernatural light.

23

A six-year-old boy is lost in the woods north of Vancouver and he lives, lives for years, in a place where only animals survive.

— From "Seven Years," by Rayline Ulyrk, *Child Development*, edition 14, volume 33 (1996)

24

Levi rifles through radio stations, the wheel shivering with what it can feel of the road. Asleep, he can tell. Smells like compost, though Levi expected that. He looks just like the rest of them, dirty and brown.

25

And you dream of the lake at Mount Currie; you dream deep in the water as the trees around you light on fire. Then you wake slowly and the city is gone. Mountains: just black on the black sky, and when you see this it makes a whirring inside you. That's the before feeling. That's the green coming in through the air vents, that's the run. Not the Raye. Raye of warm water. Raye of the yellow and bright. Hair long like a rope, she made you go, took you quiet. You know what money is, she said. You can speak.

26

And he does look like the rest, but the rest wear crystalline tattoos up and down their arms where this kid wears scars, thick and unstitched as jet streams. An oddness in the slope of his forehead, and his weird, knotted hands — retarded or something. Poor kid. Just a sleeping bag and a thin grammar schoolbook beside him, and both of them looking beat up as hell.

27

"If you're going to the valley, you're there to pick, right? I got apples... lots of work there right... kid, or what?"

28

You called her Sister and it's true.

29

How To Study a Word By Yourself

1. Look at the word. Say it plainly, but softly, to yourself.
2. While looking at the word, say the word once more, and the letters three times.
3. Close your eyes and say the letters again, and again until you learn them by heart.

— From *Our Starland Grammar: IV* (Maple Leaf Edition, 1940)

30

A farmer found you first, kept you for a while. Not for long, the cuts were still red for the nuns to dress at St. Veronica's, their fingers light as dormice. It was from them that you learned what was safe, what was comfortable, to fill a pitcher of water and look after your bowl and spoon. All with great difficulty, and all in bald daylight. All from Raye.

"Val-ley."

31

The farm is surrounded by a tall, chain-link fence that gets locked at ten, but the pickers tend to jettison their cars and dive over anyway. Three cars left here tonight, parked tight to the ditch. Levi kills the engine — he needs his keys to open the gate — and the boy doesn't stir.

32

You step out into the driveway and the crickets pulse solid as an electric current. So loud. The sky so much higher.

THREE

33

Learning to speak is about learning a series of roles; the feral child must learn to think reciprocally. It is with words that a child's memory begins to take a straight line. A life, once recalled only in match flares, becomes a story that can be told.

— From "Seven Years," by Rayline Ulyrk, *Child Development*, edition 14, volume 33 (1996)

34

The pickers are drumming and her chest feels like it will burst. Willa leans back on the porch steps as the drum sounds reach her, quiet and round. Warm, like sounds made inside a body. She picks up her ice cream and eats.

35

"You shouldn't be out here."

"Who was that?"

"You should be asleep."

"Who was that boy, Dad?"

"Just a new picker. Needed some work."

"Why'd he walk like that?"

"Walks different, I guess."

"I guess. Well, how's he going to pitch a tent in the dark?"

"I'm serious. Inside."

36

We can use the word "recovered" to mean a few different things:
(a) to be found after being lost
(b) to regain a former condition
(c) to be covered anew

Give an example for each.

— From *Our Starland Grammar: IV* (Maple Leaf Edition, 1940)

37

After she died, Levi kept her bathroom. Willa knows it was hers because of all the little shampoo and perfume bottles in a row, and the blue, silk robe. So beautiful, embroidered with trees and flowers and hundreds of little worn-out Asian people selling things to each other in markets. Sometimes the robe smells like cloth and nothing else, and then sometimes flowers again. Tonight, flowers. The towels smell good too, but like Levi: mint, soap, stone.

The lights are too bright, though, right above the sink. When Willa looks in the mirror they leave two little holes in her eyes.

38

Man's is not a closed life, ruled and governed by a given nature, but an open one.

— From "Seven Years," by Rayline Ulyrk, *Child Development*, edition 14, volume 33 (1996)

39

"Bed. Come on, Willa."

He smoothes Willa's bangs back and kisses her there; leaves her bedroom door open as he goes.

40

The others have brought tents, trailers, vans, and tarps, but just laying out on the ground is close enough. So you find a dark spot on the hill behind camp. In the bush, but it's not too bad. All the trees lined up in their rows below, and every star too, above.

You know this sky.

41

Sometimes it feels good to go in there. It did tonight — a stretching feeling in her chest, like opening a door. She closes her eyes in the dark of her room and watches the little holes fade in her eyes.

It feels good to go in, but after, it feels different. After, she has to wait. And when the door does finally close up again, she can sleep, but when she does sleep it's her mother's dream. A bad, bad, lonely dream.

But there's a cure.

42

It was there, in those years of his forehead against mine, that we began to communicate. Seated together on the cot that he crept beneath at night, he would offer his hands for me to press between mine.

— From "Seven Years," by Rayline Ulyrk, *Child Development*, edition 14, volume 33 (1996)

43

She rests her hand on the handle for just a touch — she'll just touch it. And then look around, watch the dark... nothing. She turns it barely open, pulled just so that it doesn't latch, and waits.

He's asleep anyway. She turns back and waves small, just in case, to the top of the stairs. Just to let her dad know that she's brave, and remembers him.

FOUR

44

You ran without looking and it felt good but now you've got burrs in your hair, and you can't get them out. Now you're tired, and your hands don't work. You can't get them out even though you tried to be careful and now…

45

She leaves her flip-flops on the porch, picks up her pink water bottle, and feels her way barefoot down the front walk to the driveway. Stretching, her chest stretching, and it already feels better. Her eyes clear. To the barn, now, and farther. She's walking up that hill to the top tonight, to see everything. To feel the sun first.

46

Burrs everywhere, Raye, little white ones that glow, and they hurt, too.

47

There is a small kitchen area built into a shed beside the camp. The walls are made of long boards and the spaces between boards, and even up close Willa can only see them as bands of light tonight. The pickers inside move back and forth, the black tongues of their shadows licking those spaces across. She stays close to the wall of the barn. The crickets so loud she can barely hear the voices, and she watches as the pickers stub out their cigarettes on the soles of their shoes.

Farther.

48

There were years of routine, of prayers and walks to the butcher's. Soon there were more years on two legs than four. Slowly, one by one, the hisses and bared teeth edged out into words.

— From "Seven Years," by Rayline Ulyrk, *Child Development*, edition 14, volume 33 (1996)

49

Past the camp, and running now, her feet wet from the grass, she's almost there, where the hills start. Still bright from the stars. She's stepped on something sharp but keeps going — it's okay. The house just little lights now, and the pickers all far. The stars sliding down and right into her.

50

She sees you now, and stops. And you stop.

51

There's his sleeping bag. Willa's first reaction is admiration so strong that it's hot. That's his bed — this boy is going to sleep here tonight. Here in the dark where there is nothing and no one.

Willa can't even sleep in her safe little room and this boy can just lie down and dream on the ground, on an empty hill. She stares at his sleeping bag, and the burrs in his hair. Burrs all over him like a dog, and he's pulling at them. But when she walks closer he tries to stay very still.

"Your hands don't work too good, do they?"

52

Maybe Mom is here, up in the trees. Willa searches the leaves, the moon behind them. She smiles her brave smile, just in case.

But she knows they're alone. Little lights all over. His eyes big and ugly and too wet, his teeth horrible. But his face wrinkles all up in a nice way, somehow. Something jumps in her, and it doesn't land until he looks away.

"You look thirsty," Willa says, and before she knows he is doing it, he reaches out to gently pull on her ear. It feels like a relief — like he's going to produce a quarter, and then this will all feel a little more normal. But when he takes his hand back empty, she gets a sick feeling.

FIVE

53

The water jumps up ready for oatmeal and Levi pours it in. Willa watches the back of him; she likes seeing how big he is. He's usually all folded up, to talk to someone or other, but when he stands up tall he's gigantic, and thin as a dime. Stirring the pot in that careful way of his.

"You want toast?"
"Sure, with butter."
"With butter what?"
"Sorry. Please."
Levi unwraps some butter from the fridge but it tears the bread as he tries to spread it.
"There's soft butter in the cupboard, Dad. There."
"Okay..."
"Yeah, there."

54

He saw them up there, through the window. Her little white T-shirt.

55

Could the Earth support all the things that are born?

— From *Our Starland Grammar: IV* (Maple Leaf Edition, 1940)

56

Levi brings two bowls from the stove to their paired crewel placemats, laid neatly across from each other on the table. It's late today for breakfast. Willa looks out the window; the sky so bright. She can see her bike from here, lying out on the ground by the tractors. Levi says the pickers steal everything — it doesn't matter if it's from him, or the grocery store, or each other. But not in the daylight. She'll put it away later.

She grabs an apple from the bowl on the table and takes a bite without turning. Right from the tree and she can taste the growing, the reaching from ground to apple to sky and then back again. The speed, the falling, back to the centre of the earth.

"Grace? It's your turn."

Willa bows her head automatically, steam rising between them. "For what we are about to receive…" And they eat, quietly, in the hum of the fridge. That old, hollow feeling. Both of them tired.

57

She thought you said "rain" so kept looking at the sky. Asked you what happened to your arms and when you rubbed them like that she laughed…

But you did okay. They said you couldn't be trusted to live alone, work, but they didn't think of this: the middle ground of the orchard. Only Raye. They were afraid you'd leap away again, to suckle the hills and the cinnamon bears, but you did anyways. You're gone.

And you'll be fine.

58

At breakfast he asks but there's nothing to tell. The boy didn't even talk, really. He just made a strange sound.

His scars like nets holding him all together, his joints loose and pulled on. Those weird eyes in the dawn light; a holy feeling like coming upon a nest of baby birds, or a dead body on TV that looks like it's just sleeping.

59

And soon you'll come down and the man will show you the trees and the apples, the bins, the buckets with which to fill them and the small bud by the leaf that must be left intact. When you talk, it'll sound strange, but he'll show you your row and you'll both point and nod silently, like men, and he'll leave you to finish clearing the west half of the branches.

This is your row now, your trees; these are your hands with the hard skin peeling. Your hair all smoothed nice.

60

Willa puts on her blue flip-flops and walks down the front lawn again to the fruit stand. The crickets quiet now, spark-jumping in front of her as she walks, and the new sun long and yellow on her back. Shoppers already; they drive up every Sunday in their clean, colourful cars, and their new clothes that crumple like paper around them. They've come for peaches and pears, gala apples, laid out neatly in rows. Cicadas shrill and Willa pauses to count the seconds, her mouth moving.

I'm upside down. Please turn me over.

DEAR Canada Council

© Emily Holton, 2008
First Edition

Edited by Maya Merrick
All drawings by Emily Holton

Many thanks to Maya Merrick and Christina Palassio for their beautiful edits.
The cover and the drawing on page 2 is based on designs by George Salter. The caption on
page 16 is by Pablo Neruda. Part of the caption on page 39 is from *The Epic of Gilgamesh*.
Part of the caption on page 76 is from Psalm 98:8. The turkeys on page 12 are drawings of
the following children, from left to right: Arden, Liam, Amaera, and Keegan. Some of the
phrases used to describe the narrator's visions are borrowed from Estelle Faguette's
Autobiography and Account of Fifteen Apparitions by the Seer.

Library and Archives Canada Cataloguing in Publication

Holton, Emily, 1980-
        Dear Canada Council ; Our starland / Emily Holton.

Two novellas, with illustrations, on inverted pages.
ISBN 978-1-894994-36-1

        I. Title. II. Title: Our starland.

PS8615.O482D32 2008   C813'.6   C2008-905849-6

Dépot Legal, Bibliothèque nationale du Québec
Printed and bound in Canada by Gauvin Press. Distributed by Litdistco: 1-800-591-6250

conundrum press
PO Box 55003, CSP Fairmount, Montreal, Quebec, H2T 3E2, Canada
conpress@ican.net   www.conundrumpress.com

conundrum press acknowledges the
financial assistance of the Canada
Council for the Arts toward our
publishing program.

Canada Council for the Arts   **Conseil des Arts du Canada**

DEAR Canada Council

Emily Holton

a conundrum reversible book

For DCY

Belize is for lovers!

Dear Canada Council,

My intention:

Is to do my best, never to waiver. It's to be selfless; to be a selfless person sure in her selflessness. I have been snipping at my boyfriend about things that don't matter. I ask him questions to which I already know the answers. I stamp my feet on the way up the stairs, and am slow to descend. I don't know why I'm acting this way, like an unhappy wife in a movie. But unhappy wives don't know what they need.

I am a powerful person.

My intention is to found a town.

Caye Caulker:

Is basically a sand bar over a limestone shelf off the coast of Belize. I think there is only one town on the island. According to Wikipedia, over thirty hotels are already well established there, and a number of restaurants and shops. I am confident that the existing infrastructure is perfectly adequate and requires no further augmentation from me.

My point is:

There's room. Don't think about details, Canada Council. Think about papayas. Think of mangoes. The sound of them falling as they're dumped in the bins; hundreds of musical, little wooden sounds as they land, fall in together, over and over and over again. Think of birds swallowing water, and light moving across the underside of windowsills. Think of violins, far away, slow and minor.

Fruit is the only ethical food, Canada Council. You will kill a vegetable by eating it but relieve a tree of its fruit and that tree will thank you. *Eat fruit and you steal nothing.*

Even the poor will bury their dead.

11

And I'm told they can make a passport photo in just minutes!

My point is:

Canada Council, I know what I need. I need your help. I need plane tickets.

And I am in love.

Miguel:

Miguel stole the sun and put it in the sky. He can catch a cricket with one hand, right out of the air. He can kill a deer just by running it to death.

Miguel:

Miguel was taught to be right-handed, but remained left-footed, and shoots hockey from the left. A doctor told him once that if he were to start again, his body would probably work better as a whole if he had stuck to his natural dominant side.

In the same way:

I think I'm nocturnal.

Miguel in a slim Calvin Klein undershirt playing an ancient stringed instrument.

And now, a small anthology of my sorrows.

Some background:

I haven't slept in the dark since 1987 — the summer that I was eleven.

It was a big summer:

I caught scarlet fever, evoked Brian Linehan in a dream, and as a result learned what it was that my life was for.

More background:

I grew up alone, in a small family of deaf-mutes. We lived in Hamilton, Ontario, but my parents were from Chelsea, Quebec. I'm not sure if we were francophone, but my TV was anglo. So naturally that tipped the scales for me.

Hamilton Harbour doesn't smell as bad as everyone thinks.

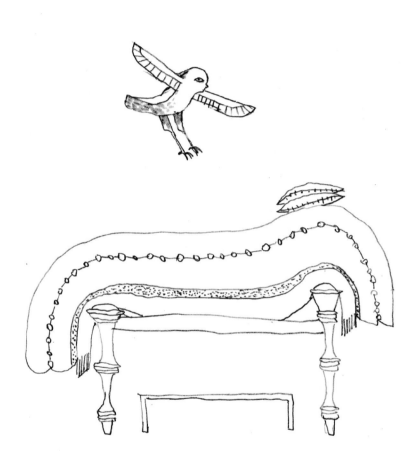

There were strange sounds in the house, that only I could hear.

19

In-depth, yet courteous, questions were his specialty.

More background:

Brian Linehan was a Canadian television host, from Hamilton, too. I always knew who he was because I saw him on TV, but also, his aunt lived next door to us.

Just because her nephew was famous she felt a little famous too. She took green pills because she was "battling depression," and then pink ones to "dissolve her farts."

My mother:

Was a twin, and read nature books. Descriptions of animal calls were always of interest to her, but it was in the spring that I was eleven that she opened the *Hamlyn Pictorial Encyclopaedia of Insects* and found —

Her North Star:

Black and shining. She marked the page with a pencil and called me to her by clapping her hands.

Yes, I could catch her a cricket. Yes, another.

And another after that.

I trust myself to see this through.

I am a powerful person:

I am a failure in my life; in many ways I have failed. And I am horribly crabby these days but I am also in love. I love straight through and bruiseless, winding my tea string around the handle. Hamilton, yet I love.

There is no mountain.

Crickets:

Will eat anything. They will crawl into your underwear drawer and eat all the little daisies out. They will breed. You can learn to be nocturnal; you don't need to be born that way. You just pick it up. I picked it up like _that_.

"Aren't you finding it a little noisy?" I asked my father once, after breakfast. I kept my hand over my mouth as I spoke so as not to offend mother, but as a result had to repeat myself, twice.

He didn't answer, but that was normal. I waited as they both sipped their tea. Both my parents were small and dark, like starlings, and you had to pick your moments with them. You had to keep still, even on the inside.

"Noisy at night?" I called out from under the table, pretending to have dropped my fork. Mother's skirt pocket was moving. He tapped his green and white cup with his fingernail, and her skirt started to fold as the crickets moved up her thigh...

I know I said they were all deaf-mutes, but my father wasn't really. Not technically deaf — just very quiet. I had some ideas on how to trap the crickets, and had prepared a few preliminary diagrams, but he just looked at me and changed the cross of his legs. And then he turned his head to watch my mother as she walked outside.

That's sign language. It means, "No, not really."

By June:

Her shifts stretched longer than daylight. Every day, by the well, or the tall grass of traffic islands. Every day, she would not clear the dead from her pockets and my father worked almost constantly, now forbidden from cutting the lawn.

I marked my own height on the doorframe and signed up for day camp, but never went.

Brian Linehan:

There were two Brian Linehans — no, three. The Brian on TV. The Brian of the Backyard. And then *my* Brian, the Apparition of Brian, the one that came to me in my sickness and saved my life, told me to work, his whole body ringing with the seven rays of fire.

The Brian of the Backyard was quiet. In real life, on the front walk, he took tiny steps, and coughed real quiet and high. He was less like TV and more like a new baby bird, just being born.

He would visit on Sundays. Sometimes, after lunch, he would cross the peonies to see to me while his aunt cleaned up. He was quiet as an Indian. I never knew he was coming until he was right there, hitching his white pants to crouch beside me in the grass. He was pale pink and gentle, and when he finally did speak I would answer just by moving my lips.

"Who?"

I shaped the word again, but slower so he could see.

He understood this time. "Oh, your mother, okay."

We were quiet again. I liked how he smelled: transparent soap, geranium leaves, rye.

"Does she know that you're watching her?"

I hesitated. We were in mother's plain view — we were right there. And yet… it was hard to explain. I shook my head.

I knew already that Brian Linehan was famous. I had seen his show many times; he was warm, calm, intelligent, and super-gay. He often astonished celebrities with what he knew about their lives. He could draw connections between personal details with an almost eerie precision.

He smiled at me. As he crossed back over to his aunt's territory, I pretended not to notice and busied myself by counting silently on my fingers a few times. But he was already gone. I wasn't beautiful or smart like the actresses he knew, and he knew it. So Brian Linehan did not return, in body, for the rest of the summer.

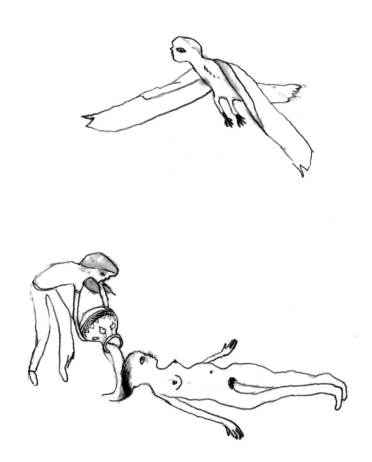

Mother told us what day she would die, and used to count the days.

Weeks passed:

Increasingly fearful of cricket injury, my mother pared down her hip and leg movements to almost nothing.

By July:

The crickets grew in number; they rang out to me, throbbed. I was a child and yet no one's province. My *Big Backyard* magazine arrived with a summer checklist of "Plants and Flowers to Know." So I worked on that, as hard as I could, for fear of not doing enough.

And also, I caught German measles.

It was in a fever that summer that he came to me — an Apparition of Brian Linehan.

It was midnight, the day of Saturday, August 31st. September 1st was commencing. It was then that the Apparition of Brian appeared and said to me, "You will either die or recover." He told me, "You will suffer and will not be exempt from pain."

Graces fell like drops of rain from his hands. I was aware of my nothingness.

There are some things I don't understand. But at least I know what happened.

This is what happened:

I was cured.

There are no stars in Hamilton:

Miguel tells me this at breakfast, as if this clears up some kind of mystery.

I know:

So I don't answer. But later, in bed, I feel sorry so I wake him just a little. Just enough so he can hear me and then I describe for him the smoke in a Caye Caulker night. The sage and rosemary, the guava shells burning red. I tell Miguel we will make love on the wing, like swifts, and explain the importance of a travel allowance.

Canada Council, I need a travel allowance.

Bad dreams.

More background:

I didn't have to sleep. I remained full of wonder. I had evoked Brian Linehan in the depths of my misery, and he had obtained for me a complete cure.

I knew I had work to do, but didn't know what it was. But I also knew that he would find me again.

In the day:

I did not go out with the others, and preferred to stay with mother. We lay down, mostly. But at night, she slept for real, and I waited alone.

Is always on, always. And if not, MovieTelevision — or it was when I was a kid. Up alone in the no-stars of 1987, I learned about the world and its workings. Remember Baby Jessica? She fell down a well in Texas and they couldn't get her out — not even the police. I couldn't believe it. I would not and could not believe that I could be safe in my house, safe in the Light of Linehan with my TV, and my blanket, and my tin roof ice cream, while at that very moment Baby Jessica was at the bottom of a well, alone, even smaller than me. _At the bottom of a well._ I watched every night, spellbound.

She was saved, though, somehow, and her toes removed. We pressed on then to brushfires and their units of small, red planes. To witnesses shading their eyes with their hands. I watched it all; became expert. Expert in car crashes, abductions, and agonized screeching… to this day my internal clock cannot be healed.

But it wasn't until two weeks later that Brian returned and told me why.

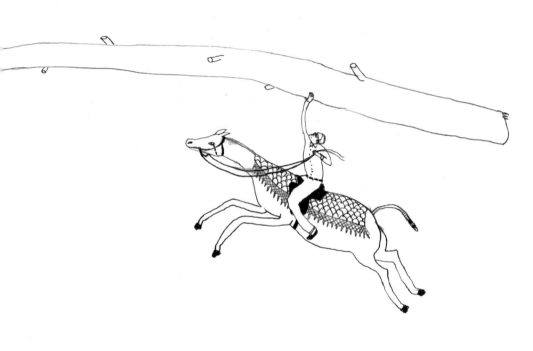

CityTV's Mark Dailey cuts down a cedar that is tall enough to make a whirlwind as it falls to earth.

39

She could read the signs in the flames of a fire, or the way a plant grew.

Audric Parent:

I want to tell you about him but you won't believe it. So Google him. Google Audric Parent and you will see. Make sure you've clicked "pages from Canada" because there was an Audric Parent in France who tried to assassinate Jacques Brel. And then there is the small mining town of Au-Parent with the streets that fall in — this is a different one. This is Audric Parent from British Columbia. That very one.

Audric Parent:

When they found Audric Parent, they put him on the news. And when I saw him, I knew. I just knew. He was mine; he would be for me. His rolling eyes, his skin, his little grey sweatsuit. All the miracles of the underbrush would happen between us.

I was ready:

They showed how he walked on four legs, and I imagined his smell. Peat and sweat, like Doritos, but in a good way. Very good. And under those sweatpants I knew: two thighs, with hair on them. I was eleven, but ready. I knew I was in love.

The crickets cheered and formed his name for me, on the coffee table, in black.

Feral children sleep in the day and so do I.

In Vedic astrology, red coral represents Mars.
In Incan astrology, it will represent me.

Possible town names:

Little Reunion, Fort Reunion, Branch of Brian's Planting.

More background:

Before the stillness overtook her, my mother taught me about the stars. She loved Orion, the hunter, and near the end she took a pen and drew his arrows all up both her arms. That was when she was signing so slow it was hard to keep track, but —

I remember:

I remember she said that in life, in real life, his arrows were made of gold. Not like in the stores, not like the diamond-heart-pendant kind of gold, but *real* gold, gold dug out of cold water, the kind of gold you swallow in flakes to cure broken bones. The kind you find underground in hard veins — she said that if a big rain came and the ground eroded all away we'd find a hard net of this rough, damp, gold, holding us up out of the sky. Her fingers would flutter and fall then, I think to represent people. All jumping off the gold net into infinity.

That's just the way my mother talked. Always beautiful, always wrong. But I remember. Everyone says I was too young to remember her but I do.

I remember her perfectly.

Like being stuffed with hot, black stones in order to be cooked.

November 1, 1987:

The day that she died was hot even early in the morning. Hot in the grass, like being cooked. Father woke me and took me out to show me that she had fallen. We stood there, in the grass, for a long time.

That night:

I awoke in the evening and Brian was there. My eyes fell upon his heart, which refreshed my mind and enflamed my inner being.

I awoke in the evening and Brian was there and while speaking to me, he extended his hands, from which fell an abundant rain. When he spoke he raised the small piece of lambswool cloth he was wearing on his breast. I had seen the small cloth without knowing what it was because it had looked white to me. But that night I saw it was the palest pink, like the shadow of a rose.

Lifted up:

I could see through his heart. Right down to the bottom. Long fish moving like wind, rocks never meant to be seen, and five long sticks of light, illuminating nothing.

And beneath:

Tiny and red, all bent up and dirty: a boy. The coyote sounds he made as they carried him; calling out sad, like a baby. What took place in my heart is impossible to tell. My thoughts were tumbling over. Brian had spoken with his heart and I had understood what he had told me. I now knew how to carry out my work in the world — my work for Audric. I wanted to suffer for him. For them both.

I wanted to suffer a great deal.

Now is the time.

Today, I watched the otters hold hands again on YouTube and I wept.

In real life:

Audric hasn't flourished as he should have. He is still in a home, some-where in BC. I keep track from little sound bites, and clips of him so thin. Foster home transfers, abuse —

So Canada Council, tell me this:

The ones who die, who aren't saved, what is their task? *I don't know.* Audric Parent grew up in the forest. He lived in places that humans are not supposed to live and when they found him he walked on four legs. This kid doesn't need rehabilitation. He just needs a place to go — the kind of place where he can write with his left hand, if you know what I mean.

I can fix this.

In Belize:

Though I won't tell them about Brian Linehan, I will tell them what he taught me, and Audric and the townspeople will find him in their own time, in their own ways.

He will be there.

Miguel:

Every tooth small and precise in his mouth, he is beautiful. He is a good man, Canada Council, studying coral, algal blooms and salt-water invertebrates. All to help me plan. *All to help me plan.* He has shown me the hydra and the many small copies of itself, growing right inside its own walls. There, the copies grow, and mature, and when they are ready they just break off and are swept away. He makes me photocopies of this, labelled in purple pen. He says my heart is a hydra, and shows me. But he's not from here, and for that reason says "heart" like "art."

"This little art wants to go," he says, tapping the paper with his pen. "One of these little arts of yours," he says. "We just need to help it grow."

Quickly, please:

Because it's hard on him, Canada Council. He shouldn't need a book on the ocean to understand my heart. He deserves precision, centricity, and if I don't finish this — all of this — I will lose him.

Too many little rooms in my heart, too many cries in the night. He is so *reasonable*, so reasonable and it's like all that calm in him makes a hole for me to fill with *un*reasonable, with obsession and wanting and Audric Audric Audric and yes, Miguel adjusts, but if we could just get to a place with some air, a light wind, the two of us could put that boy upon it and let him be okay. I could do my work for Audric, for Brian, and then it will be done and I will be empty — not in a bad way. In a good way. I want a heart like Miguel's — like an arrow, or a sail. A track jacket, with no pockets. It sounds like I'm being cute. But Canada Council, believe me.

I'm not cute at all.

Babies will be held every day!

The town:

Will be right on the shore. It will arise overnight, as if by magic. But I will build it. I will be tireless. I will found a town and I will bring in townspeople, I will find Incas to live there and work and they will fill the town with their beautiful art and folk wisdom and stories. They will sing the stories, and draw them, and create intense, tiger-striped miniatures. It will be a kind of renaissance and we will take care of each other, and we will sleep in the sand, like dogs.

So when I say I need Incas, what I mean is that I need art students, parking-booth operators, geologists from all over the world who don't have that much on. The best minds, the emptiest schedules. They can come and tell Audric's story, to each other, to their children. That's what I mean, a population. I call them Incas because they will make gold for me. The Incas will come to my town, and I will provide them with a mythology, and that mythology will start with Audric. They will tell his story, and then they will retell it, and that way they will make with it something new. New in the island of Caye Caulker, new among the roots of mangroves so thick that a rabbit will scarcely be able to walk through.

I'll also need a sash, a red mayor's sash. Or, I just need the silk — the Incas will sew it for me, with the help of whatever local peasants wish to be involved.

I need these things from you, Canada Council:

And I tell you what you will get.

Innovation!:

This is the next step. This, Canada Council, *this* is modern art. Let me make something, something beautiful, something big and alive by the ocean. Let me build it for a boy I've never met.

Enterprise!:

Stupendous evidence of toil and enterprise!

Our arrival!:

A commemorative medal of the scene will be struck of Miguel, Audric, and me, with the inscription, *Daringly performed.*

Inauguration!:

This is where you come in. I think I can afford to get the town going. There is no overhead, really — I think you can leave that to me. But three plane tickets will be tricky, and I've already mentioned the travel allowance. And then there are the dancers. I absolutely cannot afford the dancers — from Hungary — I need them and I need their costumes and I need their Furioso horses.

A multicultural affair!

Hey, Canada Council, I know you like that sort of thing. I know that turns you on. Let's get moving — let's make this happen.

Women will not have to sail if they don't want to.

The stars:

The stars are closer in Belize, by degrees. They will bring us closer to our destinies. I can't wait any longer. I need to find Audric, and tell him what I know. What Brian has told me, and Miguel has proven. And I need, every night, for my townspeople to gather wherever I am, by the water. I will unleash the dancers and horses and the Incas will know to start singing then, and then: I will tell them what Brian has told me too. I will listen to their songs and then I will tell them too.

All of it lit by the moon, and the fires, and the lights from the ships used to haul precious timber. I will do it in a whisper, but a stage whisper — everyone will hear. We'll all just be still and just listen. Our eyes open. Up at night, the children too. All of us listening.

The stars:

I know that our actions are recorded in the stars. Like destiny, but the past. I do things and the stars are changing according to what I do. They are. And Miguel's eyes change when he's sleeping, into brown speckled eggs. Warm in their dark nests they roll, pushing thin lids like two tongues against two cheeks... I hold my breath. I always wanted to be a hippie, but a hippie with a job so I could afford to go to Burning Man, like, every year. Now I type really fast, and don't have to look at my hands. Now I want to be Cate Blanchett. Now I want to be thin. Now I want to marry Miguel — I really do — and then we'll be married and maybe one day have a little Caye Caulker baby and I think about that and it feels good. Just the three of us, in our three little track jackets. Effective. Precise. Our baby will be brave and bright, and she will live in the wilderness among us, and become an archer.

The bottom line is, Canada Council: *we need to get Miguel on a plane.* Yes, he adjusts, but he also hasn't spoken all day and if we wait too long I'm afraid he won't come. So we need to get moving here because he is essential. *Essential.* I need three tickets.

In Caye Caulker, I will keep my hair in big curls, like Kirstie Alley.

Hans Christian Andersen was so worried and plagued with anxieties about being buried alive that he sometimes propped a note by his bed that read: *I only appear to be dead.*

I prop up a note that says: *I can't sleep, but I want to.*

Brian Linehan's ashes were scattered outside the Toronto home he had shared with a long-time partner, who had committed suicide two years before. He left his estate to the Brian Linehan Charitable Foundation, which attempts to raise the profile of Canadian talent and supports the creation of a Canadian star system.

He died in June of 2004. No babies were born that year.

He will be there:

And he will see us in our victory and he will love us.

*Sailfish have been seen to "run" along the surface of the water for over 200 feet,
using nothing but their wriggling tails to support themselves.*

I wish I was under there and could have caught you.

My mother:

Will be a constellation, I'll let her rest. I will work with the Incas and we will find her a place in heaven.

Smoothing her skirts and smelling of tamarisk, smelling of cedar, she will rest.

My father:

Like weather, like air. He could be in their mythology too; I could offer him to the Incas. I think he would have liked to be tall, and so perhaps he could figure as a giant in their mythology, or some kind of important tree. Or he could be the sky and hit them with lightning so that they can't go on in their lives, can't move away... I imagine his story written like a play, with no dialogue. To be performed alone, in secret. A buckram affair with just stage direction and lighting... perhaps it could be part of the Inca's puberty rites, a kind of vision quest.

My father:

Combed his hair so much that it all fell out. But we'll start way before that. We'll start his story in the womb.

We will abolish human sacrifice.

We will perform successful surgery.

My idea:

No one knows how Audric ended up in the woods, and him least of all.
The Incas will come up with some kind of wonderful, folksy explanation
— a crack in the sky, a stone thrown through. A swan, a white swan, but
shot with iridescent blue. They will name a pearl after it. And it will come
and land beside Audric and they will kiss. And when the Incas act it out
in their public squares and courtyards there will always be an old woman
there; a woman always dressed in red. She will be specially trained to leap
up at the end, every time, to throw gold flakes into the air and declare:
Triumph! The sure triumph of beauty over disaster.

And when Audric passes, in real life, light as tumbleweed in the moon-
light, we'll call to him but leave him alone and his heart will be lighter
every time. Perhaps he'll keep a den, with shit and the remains of small
animals all around, but I won't mind. I won't bother him. It's natural. But
when he wants me to, sometimes, I'll come find him and just fold up real
small beside him. Just when he wants me to. Fold up just like a sweater or
a baby fawn — barely there. And we'll rest.

Maybe the Incas won't tell of mother at all. Maybe the story will be about
how my father found a special animal and killed it. Why it needed to die.

Then her ghost crawled up into the stars and stayed there.

And every night we will gather:

To hear again, as I tell them, what Brian has told me —

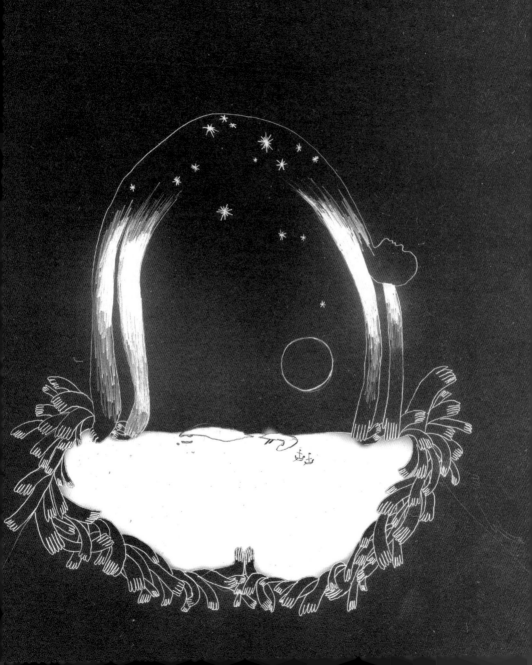

Belize's famous diving deer — let the rivers clap their hands!

We are only unwanted when we are children:

There's a whole long life after that.

Listen:

Maybe you don't know how many reds are swimming right now under water in the reefs of Caye Caulker. *Hundreds*. And I haven't yet mentioned the unharnessed possibilities for reflected light.

And Miguel says:

He will come.

Heart-whole, he will come.

Three tickets!

And Miguel understands:

Miguel understands everything, and my heart most of all. Miguel, heavy-chested and sturdy. Miguel and his excellent hearing. Miguel and me. Miguel and me and waterdogs and drums and maybe at some point a baby. Effigies of animals, created to burn in ceremony. Drums and the ocean, the water dissolved in the air. Alone with our breath and the ground in the dark alone, the moon will chip out the black water, exposing the white layer beneath and there will be stars above us too. Stars everywhere and we'll close our eyes to them. We'll close our eyes together. And we'll sleep.

I'm upside down. Please turn me over.